Dear Parents,

Welcome to the Scholastic Reader series. We have ... years of experience with teachers, parents, and children and put ... into a program that is designed to match your child's interests and skills.

Level 1—Short sentences and stories made up of words kids can sound out using their phonics skills and words that are important to remember.

Level 2—Longer sentences and stories with words kids need to know and new "big" words that they will want to know.

Level 3—From sentences to paragraphs to longer stories, these books have large "chunks" of texts and are made up of a rich vocabulary.

Level 4—First chapter books with more words and fewer pictures.

It is important that children learn to read well enough to succeed in school and beyond. Here are ideas for reading this book with your child:

- Look at the book together. Encourage your child to read the title and make a prediction about the story.
- Read the book together. Encourage your child to sound out words when appropriate. When your child struggles, you can help by providing the word.
- Encourage your child to retell the story. This is a great way to check for comprehension.
- Have your child take the fluency test on the last page to check progress.

Scholastic Readers are designed to support your child's efforts to learn how to read at every age and every stage. Enjoy helping your child learn to read and love to read.

> **—Francie Alexander**
> Chief Education Officer
> Scholastic Education

To Jonathon
—Aunt Gracie

ISBN 0-439-43992-2

Text copyright © 2003 by Grace Maccarone.
Illustrations copyright © 2003 by Norman Bridwell.
All rights reserved. Published by Scholastic Inc.
SCHOLASTIC, CARTWHEEL BOOKS, and associated logos
are trademarks and/or registered trademarks of Scholastic Inc.

Library of Congress Cataloging-in-Publication Data is available.

10 9 8 7 6 5 4 3   03 04 05 06 07
Printed in the U.S.A. 23 • First printing, September 2003

MAGIC MATT ™
and the Jack-O'-Lantern

by **Grace Maccarone**

Illustrated by **Norman Bridwell**

Scholastic Reader — Level 1

SCHOLASTIC INC.
Cartwheel BOOKS ®

New York Toronto London Auckland Sydney
Mexico City New Delhi Hong Kong Buenos Aires

Hello! I am Magic Matt.
I can do magic.

See me make a jack-o'-lantern!
Zap!

No. That is a
jack-in-the-box.
I want a jack-o'-lantern.
Zap!

No. That is a boy.
I want a jack-o'-lantern.

"Hello," says the boy.
"I am Jack."

I do not zap Jack away.
I want to be friends.

"I have some magic seeds,"
says Jack. "Let's plant them."
And we do.

The seeds grow and grow
and grow and grow
and grow and grow
and grow and grow.

"Wow!" says Jack.
"We have to climb that!"
I agree.

Up we go to a
puffy white cloud.

On the cloud is a giant castle.
We go inside.

And we see a giant
jack-o'-lantern.
"That's the jack-o'-lantern
I wanted," I say.
"It must be for me."

We take the jack-o'-lantern.
That is a mistake.

A very scary giant chases us.

We drop the jack-o'-lantern.

But the giant keeps coming.

We go down the plant.
The giant does, too.

I hope my magic works now!
Zap!

The giant is gone.
The plant is gone.
Jack is gone.

And here is the jack-o'-lantern
I wanted.

But I miss Jack.

Where could he be?

"Here I am," says Jack.

Magic Matt's Magic Words

Jar, jam, jack, jelly,
jet, jiggle, jog, and just
all begin with the letter "j".

Read these other words that
have the "j" sound, but begin
with the letter "g".

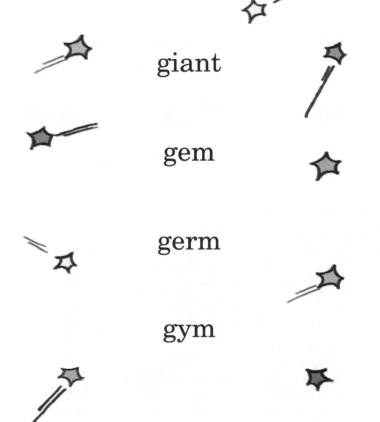

giant

gem

germ

gym

Fluency Fun

The words in each list below end in the same sounds.
Read the words in a list.
Read them again.
Read them faster.
Try to read all 12 words in one minute.

lap	back	bake
map	Jack	cake
nap	pack	lake
rap	sack	make

Look for these words in the story.

no	that	have
	boy	friends